Kimi
and the Watermelon

Kate Kidd.

June 1990

Kimi
and the Watermelon

Miriam Smith

Illustrated by David Armitage

PUFFIN BOOKS

To Kirsten Maire,
my mokopuna

Kimi lived with her grandmother
and her Uncle Tau in a little
house in the country.

Spring had come. The apple tree in the paddock was covered with pink and white blossom. The water in the creek was getting warm, and Kimi and Uncle Tau often went fishing for eels, or swimming.

Uncle Tau was going away to the city. He had worked hard digging the garden to make it ready for planting.

Together, Kimi, Grandma and Uncle Tau had planted kumara, tomatoes, onions and corn. The shoots of the young corn were already standing up like tiny blades of grass.

Uncle Tau had a special plant, a watermelon, growing in a pot.
Kimi and Uncle Tau loved watermelon. "We can plant it out in
the garden just before I go on Saturday," said Uncle Tau.
Kimi didn't want to think about Saturday when Uncle Tau
would be leaving her and Grandma.

Saturday came. Grandma looked sad as she ironed Uncle Tau's shirts. Kimi helped her fold them and put them in his bag. When Uncle Tau came out dressed in his new clothes he looked very different — not like the Uncle Tau who took Kimi eeling in the creek.

"Come on, Kimi," said Uncle Tau. "Let's plant our watermelon before the bus comes." They planted the melon in the sunniest part of the garden.

"Now Kimi, if you keep it watered, there should be a melon ready to eat by the time I come home. Will you look after it for me?" "Yes," said Kimi.

Kimi and Grandma helped Uncle Tau carry his bags to the gate. They stood and waited for the big red bus to come. When the bus stopped, Uncle Tau said, "E noho ra," and climbed on. They could see him waving through the back window until the bus turned the corner. Now there was just Grandma and Kimi.

The days grew warmer. It was summer. Every day Grandma and Kimi worked in the garden. Kimi carried water from the creek and carefully poured it around the plants. She took special care of the watermelon plant. Already it had a small round melon on it with skin as smooth and green as Grandma's precious piece of greenstone.

When the melon was small, Kimi would lift it gently to see how heavy it was. But as the days went by it grew too heavy to lift.

"Do you think the watermelon is ready to eat?" she often asked. Grandma always had the same answer, "It will be ready when Uncle Tau comes home."

Summer passed.
It was autumn.
Kimi helped her grandmother
dig the kumara.
They picked the tomatoes,
and laid the onions to dry
in the warm sun.

The corn was ready. Kimi remembered how much Uncle Tau liked corn — nearly as much as he liked watermelon. She looked anxiously at the melon.

The colour had changed. It was a softer green. Sometimes she sat beside it and tried to reach her arms all the way around. The melon felt warm and smooth against her face.

Grandma had picked all the apples from the tree in the paddock. "I shall put them away for the winter," she said. "WINTER! Is winter nearly here?" asked Kimi. "The days are getting colder," said Grandma.

That afternoon Kimi sat on the gate and waited for the big red bus. Perhaps it would bring Uncle Tau home. But the bus came along the dusty road and roared past her. For a long time she sat on the gate and looked down the road.

The water was now too cold for Kimi to play in the creek.
Grandma and Kimi didn't work outside any more. The leaves
of the watermelon had withered, and the big melon sat in the
garden all alone. "When will it be ready?" asked Kimi. "When
Uncle Tau comes home," said Grandma. From the window
Kimi could see that the apple tree had lost most of its leaves.
"There could be a frost tonight," said Grandma.

Kimi thought about Uncle Tau and how much she missed him. Perhaps he will never come home, she thought. That night Kimi cried when she went to bed.

When Kimi woke up the next morning Grandma was singing.
She hadn't heard Grandma sing for a long time. There was a
lovely smell of bacon cooking. Kimi looked out the window.
The melon had gone.

She rushed to the kitchen to tell Grandma. "Grandma! Uncle Tau's melon! It's gone!" Just then the outside door opened. In the doorway stood Uncle Tau. He had a big smile on his face. In his arms he carried the watermelon.

Uncle Tau put down the watermelon and hugged Grandma and Kimi. "It's good to be home," he said. "I've missed you both so much." "We missed you too," said Kimi. "Last night I thought you'd never come home." "Well, here I am," said Uncle Tau. "What a good gardener you are Kimi! This is the biggest watermelon I've ever seen."